Cosy Burrow Books

VALKYRIE ACADEMY DRAGON ALLIANCE
Book Three

SCORNED

I0585606

"In *Scorned*, Katrina Cope takes us on an adventure with Kara, who is on the run from Odin and must enter a dragon world and figure out how to survive. It's a tightly wound story with a surprise ending. Recommended!" –Kate B., Line Editor, Red Adept Editing

VALKYRIE ACADEMY DRAGON ALLIANCE BOOKS

Cosy Burrow Books

VALKYRIE ACADEMY DRAGON ALLIANCE

SCORNED

KATRINA COPE

ISBN: 978-0-6486613-2-0

Colin & Glenys ~ Thank you for the peace you supplied (with a view)

GET UPDATES & NOTIFICATIONS OF GIVEAWAYS

Would you like a FREE copy of Marked?
Visit here:

https://www.katrinacopebooks.com/valkyrie-academy-dragon-alliance

Through this link you can sign up for my newsletter and receive a FREE copy of Marked plus updates about my fantasy books, sales and notification of giveaways.

- CHAPTER ONE -

Wind thrums against my face, and I twist my head to the side to relieve my eardrums from the consistent pressure and noise. A frustrated groan carries across the void of land. Gazing over my shoulder and down the golden scales on the back of the dragon, I focus on the point we left behind. Even in the distance, I can see Odin's open mouth as he yells his disapproval. I've really done it this time.

I look back to Eir, and guilt rocks me to my core. I hope I haven't doomed her as well. I hadn't been thinking when I grabbed her arm to leave with me—it was a-spur-of-the-moment decision. My thoughts were only on removing everyone I cared about from the immediate threat.

I face front, and the wind blows noisily against my eardrums again. Goose bumps prickle down my arms and back as Elan takes us higher. The mountains shrink below, and crisp air fills my lungs as we rise and fall with the rhythm of Elan's wings.

On the left, far into the distance, Hildr rides her dragon. I hope that her actions and the timing of Odin's visit haven't endangered her too. She was only supposed to be going for a short flight then returning Drogon to his enclosure. The timing of Odin's appearance had spoiled the sneaky first flight. No one was meant to know that the dragon had left his stall. This could jeopardize the alliance with the dragons if Odin decides to rule it a breakaway. I contemplate what our next move should be.

The monotonous drone of the flapping wings calms my nerves, and I breathe in the crisp air only to have the calmness ripped away when Elan suddenly nosedives toward the ground. Eir presses her head into my back and clasps her arms around my waist more securely as I bring my legs forward and hook them around Elan's neck.

"What are you doing, Elan?" My words fall slightly short of a scream.

She peers over her shoulder at me, and I glimpse amusement in her eye. *Stop stressing! I've got you.*

My eyes are leaking tears from the pressure of the wind. "Yeah, but a little warning would be nice. And besides, there are two of us. It's a little harder to catch two of us if you fling us off your back," I retort.

She rolls her eyes. *Then you will just have to get working on the saddle, won't you? I'm not going to let you fall. You should have more faith in me. I'm great at catching.* She swerves off her path as if to prove a point. *You should know that. I have caught you a few times.*

"It still doesn't put me at ease," I say through clenched teeth.

You stress way too much. Have a little faith in your dragon. Elan sounds upbeat as usual — at times, it borders on annoying, and at the moment, it's leaning that way. My future — and possibly my friends' future — at the academy is at stake, all because I rescued Elan. If I had to relive my actions, I wouldn't have done anything differently. It doesn't stop me worrying, though.

I glance over my shoulder but can no longer see the stalls or the academy through the mountains that stand in the way. A small jolt rocks through Elan's body as she softly lands on the ground. Hildr's dragon circles a few moments later then lands next to us. I kick my leg over Elan's neck and slide down from her side, hearing a thump behind me as Eir follows.

Hildr's face beams from her flight, yet traces of worry crease her expression. "Odin's timing stinks!" she says. She pets Drogon gently on the nose, and the dragon nestles his chin into her hand—their bond grew stronger during the short flight. He sits on his haunches, and I notice that the swelling and redness of his injury is clearing, and the weeping has reduced. "What are we going to do?" Hildr's face puckers into a frown. "Eir and I had nothing to do with helping Elan escape. Although I completely support you in your actions. And I wasn't taking Drogon. I was only borrowing him for a quick flight before returning him until I needed him again." She crosses her arms. "Odin couldn't have chosen a more inconvenient time to come."

"I know. I'm sorry that you've been dragged into this. They were quick to chase me. They must've discovered Elan's absence in no time at all. I didn't think they would miss one dragon from the dungeon that quickly." I move back and prop myself against Elan's side. Her scales warm my back.

Perhaps it was that unconscious guard. Maybe he woke up and saw that he was alone in the dragon cell, and he alerted everyone else, Elan says. *Maybe I should've knocked him harder.*

I gasp. "Elan!"

Oh, don't get your tail all twisted. I'm kidding. You saw how I reacted to hurting him. I don't like hurting people. Besides, he ran into my tail, remember?

"Aha," I say, crossing my arms over my chest. "You seemed to be having a lot of fun back there, acting like a big bad dragon."

Oh, I was. Her front feet shuffle with excitement.

I glance at Eir and notice that she looks pale. "Are you okay, Eir?"

She nods with a vacant expression, staring over the wastelands. "Yeah. I'm just worried about what to do next." She pauses and twists one of her wavy light-brown locks. "Actually, I'm more worried about what Odin will do to you." Her brow pushes together in a frown, and she looks at me. "Hildr and I can go back at any time. We had nothing to do with Elan's breakout. And Odin's reasonable, right?"

I can't help but laugh. "Um, not that I've seen. I would be more likely to class him as unreasonable unless you can somehow manage to get him to see your way. It's something I haven't yet achieved."

"It's not like Hildr and I have done anything wrong. She took a dragon for a flight, but she was going to return him."

"Odin is not a peacemaker like you are," I say, "although the dragon does have to go back to the stall."

Drogon stomps his foot and shakes his horn-covered head. *I don't want to go back to my stall.*

"But you have to." I push off Elan's back and stand in front of him.

But I don't want to. He stomps the other foot. *The food in there is disgusting, and I shouldn't be held captive.*

"How is the food disgusting?" I raise an eyebrow at him.

They give us meat that is already dead and cut up. It's not fresh and running around.

Eir screws up her nose in disgust then turns the other way.

You have to return, Drogon. Elan pushes her shoulders back and uncoils her wings, giving off the impression that she is larger.

Drogon plunks himself on his backside, and a deep frown sets on his face. *Why?*

Because it is part of the alliance. If you don't go back, then you can disrupt the treaty, and it could cause a war between the Valkyries and the dragons again. We could lose many. You don't want that on your conscience for the rest of your life, Elan says, her golden-brown eyes flooding with compassion and sympathy.

But I don't want to. Drogon's bottom lip protrudes and droops slightly.

Elan stands on all four feet and towers over him. She huffs, and tendrils of smoke escape her nostrils. *You made a promise to me that you would go back. You have had your fun, and now you will go back. That is an order*. Elan's voice booms with authority, and I almost mistake her for her mother again.

Drogon's large brown head tilts forward, and his gaze falls to the ground as his front legs crumple in an act of submission. *Yes, Elan. I will go back.*

Elan sits back down and folds her wings. *Good*.

I am dumbfounded. It is the first serious act of aggression and authority that I have seen from Elan, and this time, there was no bluffing. It's as though she is the commander of her soldiers. I know she is a higher ranked dragon, but it's strange to see, given that she is usually cheerful and happy.

Hildr looks from dragon to dragon and scratches her fingers through her spiky red hair. "Clearly, I have to take Drogon back to the stalls and tie him up again. This will risk exposure to Odin, anyway." She turns to Eir. "I think you should come with me. We'll try and talk our way out of this. Perhaps we can convince Odin that you were on my dragon, not Elan."

"That's going to be dangerous, Hildr," I say.

She touches her hand to the hilt of her sword. "It's a challenge that I am willing to take. I could never cower from danger. We will work this out. After all, I am returning the dragon. The most punishment I expect is a slap on the wrist. As for you, I don't know what they would do. I don't think it will be safe for you to return until things settle down. When that happens, I'll come and find you."

"Where will you go?" Eir asks me with a strange mixture of worry and contentment.

You can come with me to the wastelands.

I never thought I would hear that said in such a cheerful voice. Then again, I didn't expect anything else from Elan.

"The dragon wastelands?" I ask.

Of course. Where else would I take you?

"Will I be safe there?" I fiddle with the strap of my quiver that lies across my chest.

Elan pushes her mouth to one side, looking thoughtful. *To be honest, I have no idea. But I will protect you.*

"But you're only one dragon in how many?"

A lot. But don't worry. I'm tough. She pulls back her lips, exposes her teeth, and growls.

My mouth twitches up at the side. "For some reason, that doesn't put me at ease."

- CHAPTER TWO -

A knot twists deep in my stomach as I watch Hildr and Eir take off on the back of Drogon. The dragon has managed to hone his flying skills most of the time, although occasionally, he still tosses his passengers. I grit my teeth as Eir flops from one side to the other, but eventually, Drogon learns to correct himself and catches her. Eir wraps her arms around Hildr and straightens her back. A deep sadness fills her face as she glances over her shoulder at me, causing the strings to pull tighter on the knot in my stomach. I can tell she is concerned about my safety more than her own.

I don't know what my future holds. I hope that I can work my way out of this and back into the Valkyrie world, where I can prove the worth of all the wingless Valkyries. As I watch my friends disappear over the horizon, the urgency overwhelms me, but first, I have to learn how to survive in the wastelands.

I hope that Hildr and Eir are accepted back to the academy, even if it is not with open arms.

Elan dips down, and I climb on her back, encircling her neck, yanking my legs over the top of her, then hooking my heels into her sides. As I do this, the arrows knock around in their quiver, reminding me of their existence. In all the hurry and excitement, I'd forgotten that I had slung them over my back before I raced to see if I could get to Midgard. The reaction is so ingrained in me from my training that I don't need to think about it. I reach around the back of my neck with one hand. My fingers brush the hilt of my sword, and I breathe a sigh of relief. It is secured between the quiver and my back. They may not be much, but at least I'm not entirely defenseless.

I hook my arms around Elan's neck again. "Let's do this."

Elan pushes off the ground and takes to the air. The chilliness of the air stirs up my anxiety. I haven't been to the dragon wastelands since the day I rescued Elan's egg. I had run so far that day purely by coincidence, and I'm glad I did—I saved the eggs of that nest. I survived that day in the wastelands dominated by the dragons, but that was only against one dragon. Elan's mother had made it clear that she would not spare me if she found me out there again.

We fly in silence. The wind blows against my ears, blocking out the consistent beat of Elan's flapping wings. The chill of the air raises goose bumps on my skin. I didn't realize that dragons could reach such a high altitude when they fly.

I can hear your brain ticking over. What are you think and about? Elan's cheerful voice, in stark contrast to how I am feeling, pierces my head, distracting me from the thrumming in my ears.

I expel a breath. "How can you be so lighthearted? So much is weighing on my shoulders right now. I don't have a home to go to, and I have to stay among dragons who may eat me. I'm worried."

So you should be. She peers over her shoulders, and I spot humor in her eyes.

"That's not funny. It is quite serious." I glower at Elan.

I know. But you can't worry about everything. Just take it one step at a time. She remains frustratingly cheerful.

I poke her under her scales, trying to find some softer skin. I know that she is right, but it doesn't make it any less irritating. "Since when did you get so wise? You're not even a fraction of my age, and you seem to know so much."

Ah. So we're trying sarcasm now, are we? That's okay. I know I'm smart for my age. She smirks.

I roll my eyes. A deep chill encases my arms, and I shiver.

Are you cold? The smirk has left her face.

"Freezing, actually. This Valkyrie uniform is sleeveless." I look down at my leather pants. "At least my pants are long."

She tilts her head and looks at me again. *Your goose bumps are bigger than your eyes.*

"I know. I'm the one experiencing them."

She shakes her head. *You'll have to do something about that.*

"And a saddle, remember? I'm only just hanging on here. I'm surprised I'm not warm from the effort." I pull myself forward and hook my legs around her neck. "My arms are exhausted."

Elan dips, pulling us out of the clouds. On the ground below, I recognize the small spot where I had stood that day when I faced the creature who was trying to steal Elan's egg, who had scratched me in the process and left me with the large scar on my shoulder. This is the place where I had saved Elan and her siblings and stopped Elan's egg rolling off the cliff.

See anything familiar?

"Yes, I do. How close is your nest to the other dragons?"

It's not too far. I'll show you when we land. She tilts up her wings, and we drop elevation quickly. As her feet hit the earth, her body rocks with a small thud, and she kneels close to the ground. I don't see any other dragons, and I flick my legs to one side and slide down her scales off her back. It's incredible how different the ground is here in comparison to the area around the academy, even though we're not that far away. I move around Elan, searching the area and taking in the scenery. Dragon eggshells are scattered across the ground, and they crunch under my feet.

I look at Elan. "Are these your dragon eggshells? I would have thought that your eggshells would have disintegrated by now."

Oh, mine has. These are from my younger siblings.

My mouth drops open. "You have more siblings?"

Well, yeah. Dragons lay eggs at least once a year. Mother's been busy trying to repopulate our kind. She's been doing a good job too.

"Except it has captured Odin's attention, now that she is producing more than one egg a year, and that's why he's demanding that he has one of your breed every year."

He can stick it where the scales don't grow! He's not getting me or any of my siblings. There aren't many female dragons at reproducing age, and it isn't in the alliance contract. She thumps her tail against the ground. *And Mother would never approve it.*

"That's one of the things he's upset over. And because you've agreed to be with me, I'm on the firing line." I stoop down to pick up a piece of eggshell. Its gold glitters in the sun, tainted slightly by the black, creating a beautiful contrast. I run my hand over the rough surface. A memory sparks. "Does the creature still come to steal eggs?"

There have been reports that eggs are still going missing. It's increasing the dragons' intolerance to the alliance with the winged Valkyries. Between that and the missing eggs, our population isn't growing quickly enough.

"Why can't any of you keep watch and look out for the creature?"

It's a sneaky creature. The dragons eat a lot and have to go hunting regularly. And it always seems to know when to come.

"Then why don't you designate one dragon to watch over the eggs while the other dragons go out hunting?"

Elan chuckles.

"What's so funny?"

That would mean that we'd have to get along. And that just doesn't happen among the dragons at the moment.

"Is it really that bad?"

She nods.

"Then can't your mother demand it, for the sake of the safety of the dragons?"

I know it's hard to believe, but Mother doesn't like being bossy and ordering dragons around all the time. She wants peace among the tribes.

I fiddle with the eggshell in my hands. "But this particular demand would aid peace."

I still can't see it happening.

I shake my head. "It's a shame."

The ground rumbles behind me, and I drop the eggshell and spin around to come face-to-face with an angry dragon.

- CHAPTER THREE -

Hot dragon breath coats my face as I stare into a huge mouthful of teeth—the pointy white canines are only inches away from my face. I back off, trying not to stumble over the stony surface. The dragon snorts, and tendrils of smoke escape between the gaps in its teeth. I hold up my hands in a stopping motion, hoping that they won't become the first things that get chomped off.

"Hi. I am here in peace." I continue backing away while glancing over my shoulder, checking for the cliff's edge. The arrows in my quiver rattle, but I know they won't do me any good. The dragon's golden-brown eyes glare down at me, and the farther I step away, the narrower the eyes become.

I study the dragon from head to toe and note the two large horns protruding from the top of its wide head. Its mouth is filled with spiky teeth, and drool drips from them as it stares at me as though I might make a tasty snack. The golden glint in its scales sparkles in the sun exactly like Elan's—it's another emperor dragon. I continue to back away, hoping to hide behind her. I glance sideways, looking for her, and my face clouds with worry when she seems farther behind that I expect.

The dragon's eyes seem to dance with humor. *Oh, Elan, you brought me lunch. That's nice of you.* Elan hurriedly steps in front of me, and I breathe a sigh of relief. My heart is pounding so hard in my chest that I feel as though it is going to jump out to give the dragon an appetizer before it starts on the rest of me. Their voices rattle through my head as they speak to each other.

No, Sobek. This is not your lunch. Kara is my friend, and you should treat her with respect.

Sobek grumbles as he moves closer. *She smells of Valkyrie blood, and she's in the wastelands. She's fair game.*

Elan stands firm. *No. Kara isn't lunch. You will not touch her. She's important to us.*

Blah, blah. Whatever. Move out of the way. He attempts to shove past her.

A low rumble shakes Elan's body, and a puff of smoke escapes her teeth. *This is the Valkyrie who saved me as an egg. You are not going to touch her. Mother and I have agreed to protect her, and the only way to do this at the moment is to bring her back here despite what she said about her returning.* For the second time today, Elan's voice is surprisingly firm.

Sobek slams his tail against the dirt, and the ground vibrates. *That's not fair! She shouldn't be out here if that's the case. Any Valkyrie out here is fair game.*

Elan moves aside and exposes me to Sobek again, who surveys me with hunger as distrust taints his eyes. My feet shake in my boots. Thankfully, he's not moving toward me, and Elan remains on full alert. After a few moments, Elan backs up with one of us on either side. *Sobek, this is Kara. Kara, this is Sobek. He's my little brother.*

I swallow the lump in my throat. "Ah, nice to meet you," I say with a voice full of uncertainty. I look from Sobek to Elan then back to Sobek again, almost chuckling at her calling him "little." "I assume you mean your younger brother... because he's huge."

Elan chuckles. *Yes, younger. He was in the same clutch of eggs.*

"So one of the other two eggs in your clutch to hatch after you?" I ask. "What about the other one?"

They both hatched. My mother is very fertile. That's why she's working the hardest to increase our population. It's kind of a bummer because we all seem to be related, which makes it harder to find someone to couple with who we're not related to. She nudges Sobek on the shoulder. *And because I was born before this dragon, I'm in charge of him. He's supposed to listen to me. It's not always the case, though.*

Well, you've done some pretty stupid things, Sobek says.

I'm still learning. Everyone makes mistakes when they're learning.

Like the mistake you're making right now by bringing her to the dragon wastelands? She's definitely going to be someone's lunch before the day is over.

Hopefully, no one will find her straight away. Hopefully, it will be a slow process of introducing her, and they will listen to me and Mother, their leader.

He sits on his haunches. *You know that's not the way things work at the moment. This alliance is getting their noses out of joint. You and I are lucky that we are a rare breed.*

Yeah, about that. Odin is now searching for our kind. He captured me, except Kara found out and rescued me from his dungeons. I'm indebted to her twice now. It's getting a bit ridiculous. She tilts her head at me and gives me a strange glance. *I owe her at least two lives.*

"You don't owe me anything." I walk up to her and place a hand on her front leg. "I'm happy to have you as my friend. To me, this is enough repayment."

The looks she gives me says she's unconvinced. *The day will come, I'm sure.*

I glance at Sobek again. "What happened to the other egg from your clutch?"

I have another sister too, Elan says.

"Where is she?"

Elan saunters toward the edge of the cliff and peers over. *She's down there with the rest of the dragons.*

I walk up to the side and peer over the edge with her. If I thought I was scared facing her brother, then I had no idea. The valley is full of different-colored dragons stomping around close to one another, some of them fighting openly and drawing blood. It looks wild and untamed, and suddenly, I'm nervous again. Elan is but one dragon. "Elan, there is no way you can protect me against them."

Don't worry. Sobek will help us, won't you, Brother? She nudges him with her butt, and he sways on his feet.

A low grumble rises in his throat.

See, I told you, she chirps at me.

I look at Elan in disbelief. "That didn't sound like an agreement."

Oh, don't worry. He sounds like that all the time.

Rocks clatter behind me, and I turn to see Elan's mother approaching. With her is a dragon who, if not for the dark streaks on her cheeks, would look exactly like her.

Her mother chastises her. *Elan. What are you thinking, bringing her here?*

She saved me again, Mother. Odin sedated me and locked me in his dungeon because Kara wouldn't hand me over. Eventually, Kara found out where I was, and she rescued me.

The mother's eyes land on me. Even her friendly face is intimidating. *Is this so?*

I nod. "I did it because Elan is my friend, not because I want to hold debts over her head. I like your daughter, and I'm happy to work with her. She helped me slay a frost giant and save the winged Valkyries and the academy, not to mention a large part of Asgard. I thought they would thank us and welcome me into the fields so I can help reap soldiers from the dying warriors for Valhalla. Instead, it turned out completely the opposite. Odin demands that he have Elan or another of your breed of dragons. He claims that you owe him because the emperor dragons are having more than one dragonette per year."

Well, he can't have one. It is not agreed upon in the alliance. Her voice rumbles with anger.

"I know, and I told him that, but then he stole Elan anyway. Now I've rescued her, and he's after me—that's why Elan brought me here. And to be honest, I'm scared. I don't want to be here, as much as I love dragons. Peering over the edge and seeing the turmoil that is down there makes me scared."

You should be scared. I cannot guarantee your safety. We will have to hide you here on this pedestal and hope that the dragons will not see you until things settle down. But it is best to try and go back home as soon as possible. Is anyone arguing on your behalf?

"My two friends were kind of dragged into this by accident. They have flown back—"

Flown back. Are they winged Valkyries? Her eyes fix on me, interrogating me.

"No. They have gone back on a dragon, one of the captured ones who has not been there for long."

The mother looks at Elan, and there's disapproval in her eyes. *What are you doing, Elan? This is not part of the deal.*

Right, Mother, it's not part of the deal that I made with you when we decided for me to go. If only you could see the joy that I have brought and feel the complete connection I have with Kara. Her friends have seen this and are keen to join in and help the alliance and stop the dragons being persecuted. They had a quick ride on me, and they are addicted. She giggles. *They're so keen to work with us that they are like little children.*

It sounds as though they are treating dragons like pets, the mother says disapprovingly.

I shake my head. "Oh, no. The dragons are making it clear who's in charge, although

Naga's a bit more of a pushover because he's keen to cooperate and he's so cute."

The mother dragon grumbles deep down in her throat, and a small puff of smoke exits her mouth. I'll have to remember not to call them cute next time. Clearly, the mother doesn't like it.

- CHAPTER FOUR -

We're going to have to keep out of sight and away from all the other dragons, the mother says.

Of course. We'll do whatever we can. Sobek stands at attention as though faced by a corporal.

I don't want any harm to come to her. Elan glances at me with worry in her eyes.

I'll have to go and sort this out so that we can get her out of here quickly. The leader of the dragons paces in front of us, her forehead crumpling into a frown between her horns. *Clearly, Odin needs reminding of our contract. It's going to be difficult. I have heard that his head is so thick that it's hard to speak to him.*

"That seems true," I say. "He seemed shocked when I let it drop that I can speak to you. He thought that was impossible, so I had to ad-lib."

It is impossible with him because he's so closed-minded. I'll have to go and hope that Loki is there. Then he can shapeshift into dragon form so that he can translate. She paces some more. *Most of these gods are thickheaded and too hard to speak to. Thor is one of the worst.*

I find it difficult to hold back a chuckle. We are always taught to respect the gods, and it's strange hearing them talked about in this way.

Eingana.

This voice is strange to me, so I duck behind Elan.

What is it, Ness? the highest-ranking dragon asks.

Finally, I know the mother dragon's name. I have been too intimidated to ask.

Too many dragons are down there fighting, and it is getting out of hand. No one can get through to them. We need you to step in.

Hiding behind Elan's legs, I sneak a peek. A bright-red female dragon stands in front of the leader. Her eyes are framed in black, giving her a seductive, feminine appearance. I know there are red dragons in the stalls, but their look is vastly different from the other dragons, almost as though they are making a statement. Two horns on top of her head point to the sky, except unlike the emperor dragons' horns, which are straight and solid, these horns fork off like branches on a tree in Midgard. White fur lines her eyebrows, chin, and chest, with a fluffy patch on the end of her extremely long tail. Even her back is not straight like the other dragons—instead, it is humped like a camel. Coupled with the brilliant red scales, her breed of dragon looks as though it should be on display.

Ness tilts her head and nose into the air and takes in a couple of deep breaths. *It smells like Valkyrie up here.* Her eyes narrow.

I lose all feeling in my face and pull back, standing upright and hiding behind Elan's legs. My heart thumps rapidly against my ribcage, begging to escape. This will not do. If I don't quiet my heartbeat, Ness might be able to hear it. I take slow, deep breaths, making sure the air doesn't whistle in my nostrils.

Eingana discretely moves between Elan and Ness. *Oh, that's just Elan*, she says. *I've been sending her to watch over the Valkyries and try and smooth out this alliance with them so we can stop all this bickering.* The leader of the dragons flicks her tail dismissively. *She reeks of them when she comes back.*

Ness sneers, and a long deep grumble escapes her throat. *You can say that again. The smell is overbearing. Is it working?*

Some of the wingless Valkyries are on our side, but we have a long way to go. Elan's voice is level and calm. I don't know how she is doing it.

The red dragon spits. *Valkyries are disgusting. They treat us appallingly. One of my children is held there, locked up like some kind of degenerate and used as weapons practice. I want her back.*

We're working on it, Ness, Eingana says. *It is a lengthy process. And Elan is working as fast as she can. Come, let's go and sort out this fight.* She maneuvers toward Ness and coaxes her away from our spot. Thankfully, Ness moves without too much encouragement, and they fly to the dragons below.

"That was close." I move out of the shelter of Elan's belly once I see them drop below the cliff face.

This can happen a lot if you're around here. We have to find a safe place for you.

Sobek spreads a wing, indicating a spot in the cliff face. *There is a small cave on the side of that mountain just there. It might be the best spot for you to seek shelter away from the sight of the other dragons when they fly over us.*

Good thinking, Brother! Let's go check it out. Elan stomps toward the cave and holds out her wings slightly so I can walk underneath them, hidden in case any dragons fly over. She peers at me under her wing, her face amused. *You're so tiny. I don't know why they would want to eat you for lunch. There's no fat on you.*

"Somehow, that doesn't make me feel any better." I grimace at her. A loud groan escapes my stomach.

What was that? She tilts her head to the side, giving me a strange look.

"That's my stomach. I'm starving. It's just reminding me that I haven't eaten anything since breakfast."

She ushers me into the cave, her large form barely fitting underneath. I take in the rocky formation. It's certainly not comfortable, but it is cozy. The pattering of water catches my attention, and I spot water running down the side of the rocks, welling in two different holes. Thankful to have it, I run forward, scoop up a handful of water, and drink it greedily.

Elan watches me with interest. It's in times like this that I remember that we haven't spent much time together. Each of us has peculiarities that the other is not familiar with. I finish drinking then remember my manners. "Would you like some?"

She shakes her head. *No, thank you. You stay here. I'll go out and see if I can find some food.*

Before I can answer, she takes off and leaves me alone in the cave. Despite its secrecy, I still feel insecure. I am in a strange place with no real protection against any of the dragons. A sword and a quiver of arrows are not the ideal defenses against dragons, not that I want to cause any of them harm. I still have to survive.

Time ticks by slowly, and I watch Sobek standing guard outside the cave until the monotonousness of it sends me to sleep. I am woken with a thud and tiny pebbles hitting my face. I pry my eyes open and am faced with a lifeless animal that Elan has thrown in front of my face. It's probably about half my size and much too big for me to eat alone.

I pull my sword out of its sheath and set to work, removing the skin from its flesh with the tip of the blade.

What are you doing? Elan stands over me, watching my every move. *You're cutting off one of the best parts.*

"The skin?" I pause what I'm doing and look at her in disbelief.

Yeah, the skin is delicious. Or at least the fat underneath it.

"Well, it's way too tough for us to eat, so we use it to make essential things."

Like what?

"Saddles, clothes, and weapons bags." I pause and look at her. "Do you know where to get a lot of salt?"

Sure. There is a field not too far from here that is low and hot, where salt covers the ground. We call it the death field because not a single creature lives there.

"Are you able to bring me back a fair bit?"

What for?

"So I can preserve this skin. I'm going to need it."

She huffs. *All right, but you better not be turning me into an errand dragon.*

I chuckle. "No, I won't use you as a slave. I promise. But I can't go out and get it myself."

Okay. Elan exits the cave and pushes off into the sky.

While she is gone, I finish skinning the animal then throw the skin over a boulder at the back of the cave. I wash myself off in the second puddle and take another drink from the one with the fresh water running directly into it.

A clatter of rocks sounds near the entrance of the cave, and I turn just in time to see Elan with a disgusted look on her face as she charges inside. *Where do you want it?* Her eyes look panicked, and I wonder why until I look at her mouth and see it is crusted in salt. She is holding the salt in her mouth. Yuck—no wonder she looks uncomfortable. I hadn't thought of how she would carry it.

I point to the second puddle of water, and she runs to it, spits the salt into the water, then plunges her mouth into the liquid, opening and shutting it a few times. She pulls her nose out and spits. *That was disgusting!* She indicates the first puddle with the water running into it. *Is that fresh water?*

I nod.

She dashes to the puddle and plunges her nose deep into its contents, sucking in a big mouthful. *That's better.*

I chuckle and set to work slicing off a piece of meat about double the size of my hands off the rump of the animal. I slap the piece of meat on a rock in front of Elan.

That's not going to fill me. Elan looks at the piece of meat with disappointment.

"That's not for you. It's mine. I was going to ask you to cook it for me."

She looks at me strangely. *What do you mean by cook?*

"I need you to breathe your fire over it until it is grilled enough for me to eat."

Elan screws up her nose. *Yuck! That would make it disgusting. Why would you want to burn your meat?*

"It's just the way I like it."

She shrugs then does as I asked. The smell of burnt flesh reaches my nose, and my stomach growls louder. It's nicely charred. "Stop. That's perfect."

She screws up her nose, and I shove the rest of the animal toward Elan. "The rest is yours."

Her face lights up, and she finishes the whole carcass before I finish my chunk of meat.

I wash my hands in the salty water then throw the skin into it, swishing it around a few times.

Wings flap outside the cave, and I spin around with my eyes wide.

Don't worry. It's just Sobek. He's going hunting for his meal now that I'm back to protect you.

I notice that the sun is dropping below the horizon, and darkness is engulfing its light. Elan moves farther into the cave and curls into a ball. I nestle against her body, pressing my back into her side and absorbing its heat. It's a strange, comforting feeling to be curled up with a dragon and having the heat from her body keeping away the cold of the night in the wilderness. Only a few months ago, I never would have thought it was possible that a vicious creature could turn out to be so loving and caring. Tomorrow is another day, providing I can get through the night without being eaten by a wild dragon.

I drift off to sleep only to be woken by a thump at the entrance of the cave.

- CHAPTER FIVE -

My eyes shoot open, pulling me rapidly from my sleep. I hope that the thump was just Sobek returning from his hunt. Quietly, I roll up to my feet then tiptoe to the edge of Elan's enormous body to peer around her at the entrance of the cave. My face is hit with an icy-cold breeze from the wastelands, pulling me further from my sleep. I can't see anything at the entrance, so I move closer to get a broader view. Despite the chilliness and potential danger, my curiosity gets the better of me.

As I peer out of the cave, I don't find any sign of movement. Sobek and Elan's sister lie together, asleep under the moonlight. Tiptoeing past them, I head to the edge of the cliff.

Another thump sounds behind me, and I spin around, my eyes wide. I can't see any movement. I know I am exposed, so I dart toward Sobek to take cover only to stop when his tail lifts then thwacks to the ground. Now it makes sense. He must be having a restless dream.

I release the pent-up breath and head back to the cliff edge to peer down at the dragons in the valley below. Most of the dragons are curled under the moonlight, though some still wander around. There doesn't appear to be as many dragons in the valley as there were earlier today. I squat and study them, taking in all the different colors and how they group among their own breeds.

A rock clatters behind me, and I twist around, startled. Charging toward me from several feet away is Sobek. A strange look is plastered on his face, and it sends shivers down my spine—I hope he's not charging at me to eat me when no one is looking. Perhaps he didn't catch anything to eat earlier and is still hungry. I want to run, but there is nowhere to run where he cannot get to me. Instead, I pull all my courage together and remind myself that he has sworn to protect me because of what I've done for Elan.

His great form halts extremely close to me, and something blocks the light of moon falling onto my body. I glance up to see that his wing is towering over the top of me.

What are you doing? Are you trying to get yourself killed? Dragons who can see in the dark are flying above. Walking around like this is a quick way to become dragon dinner.

I move forward a couple of steps and peer past the edge of his wing. A shadow of a dragon passes in front of the moon.

They are searching for prey naive enough to be sleeping out in the open. Many animals come out at nighttime, when it is not so hot. You're so lucky you haven't been spotted. Sobek's voice booms in my head. He tucks his head underneath his wing and stares at me. The moonlight casts harsh shadows over his eyes, making them seem more intimidating.

I gulp. "Thank you. I didn't realize. The only dragons I've had anything to do with have been Elan and the ones captured in the stalls. It's impossible to learn their habits and skills when they are unable to leave the stalls to search for their prey."

He continues hovering over me with his wing spread, sheltering me like a big mother hen warming her chicks.

I gaze back over the edge of the cliff, observing the dragons in the moonlight. "There seem to be a lot of dragons here. Are there more colonies than this? If there are, then your population must be increasing."

The population is increasing, but unfortunately not fast enough, and it's only because of the alliance we have made with the Valkyries. It would increase quicker if we didn't have to hand over one youngling every year. We could breed a lot faster if we had them here and the war between the Valkyries and dragons remained finished. He peers over the edge and sighs loudly. *But at the moment, it is causing much unrest because we have to hand over these young, knowing that they are subject to the Valkyries and their unforgiving mercy. The only thing that keeps these dragons handing over their young is because the Valkyries would attack us again if we stopped this alliance.*

I search around the top of the mountain, and I see his sister still sleeping. "Where's Eingana gone?"

Mother has gone back to the academy and to the palace to spy on Odin and the other Valkyries. She needs to see what the result is from the disturbance of your freeing Elan. And to see what the outcome will be for your friends who returned with the dragon they took. Hopefully, she will be back soon. His feet shuffle a little, as though he is moving into a more comfortable position. *After she sees what's going on, she will negotiate with Odin over the new rules that he wants to enforce on the alliance.*

He shakes his body and continues standing over me. I move in closer, leaning against his scales and soaking up their warmth. Something on the ground glistens in the moonlight, and I look down, spotting several golden scales glowing dully.

I stoop down and pick one up. It is about the size of my hand. I tap on it, my nails clinking softly against the hard surface. I poke the underside, noticing that the hard surface is not budging under my pressure. Grabbing a rock, I slam it against the scale. It doesn't give. It remains as robust as it was a few moments before. I turn to Sobek and tap against his scales with the point of the rock.

He peers down at me with curiosity in his eyes. *What are you doing?*

"I'm just checking out your scales," I say as though it is an ordinary thing to do.

Ah, why?

"Because they appear to be so hard, and I notice that there are a lot of scales of your siblings lying over the ground. Is it normal for a dragon to lose scales like this?"

Like any reptile, we shed our skin now and then. The only difference is that dragons shed a scale or two at any time, not the whole surface, like reptiles. The scales get pushed out when another one pushes through—kind of like losing teeth. That way, we only have a tiny hole exposed at any time, hindering too much damage when attacked, provided we are not hit in the vital spots.

"What can your scales withstand?"

I don't think I should tell you that. If I tell you, then you may use that information against us.

I tilt my head to the side and give him a weird look. "Do you really think I'm going to use anything against you and the dragons?"

He stands in silence.

I continue, "The only time I would use it against them is if they attacked me and I needed to defend myself. I think you guys are to be revered. I have so much respect for your kind, and I would love to see us work together, not kill each other."

He stares at me for a moment, as though trying to process the information. He nods slightly, yet his eyes don't leave me. He looks to be observing and processing information. *Very well. There is very little that our scales will not withstand. They withstand fire on the outside and trap heat when exposed to extreme cold. If we need to release some of that internal heat, we can open our scales to allow the heat to escape.*

"Do mean like how we have goose bumps?"

What are goose bumps?

"Goose bumps are when we get little bumps on our skin, and the hairs stand on end, trapping all the heat within the hairs so it holds some of our warmth."

He looks thoughtful for a moment. *I guess it is kind of like that, only opposite because we are letting the air out.*

"Clever."

It is also nearly impossible for a spear to penetrate our scales unless they manage to pierce a place that is shedding or underneath a scale and straight into the soft skin.

I pick up a scale, feel its texture, and turn it to look at the underside, feeling it there too. I notice that there is a floppy part, not as tough as the top side of the scale. This is near the connection where it would mold onto the skin.

"What about this bit?" I ask.

That is the part I am talking about. It is a little softer so it can connect.

"So this would be a perfect spot for me to sew it onto something."

He frowns. *Why would you want to do that?*

"I need protection when I am on Elan's back. Perhaps I can make something out of this, like a jacket. That way, I should be warm when we are traveling at a high altitude, and it will also act as a shield."

Then you would have the toughest jacket that anyone has ever made.

- CHAPTER SIX -

I gather several scales into my arms, carry them back to the cave, and toss them into a corner before cuddling back into Elan. My mind runs wild with all the things I could make with the scales. A chill runs down my spine, and I press my back against Elan, taking in her warmth, and fall asleep.

The next day, when the sun is high, it glistens off the rocks and shines straight into the cave. I force my eyes open. Elan is not lying next to me. I roll over and crawl to my feet, searching for any sign of her. A large figure stomps my way. I've found her, and she doesn't look happy.

Are you trying to get yourself killed? What are you thinking, wandering off in the middle of the night out into the open in the middle of the dragon wilderness? Her wings spread wide in frustration.

"I'm sorry. I didn't realize."

You do know that dragons have excellent hearing, don't you? You need to keep your voice down, she says through gritted teeth. She grabs something from the entrance of the cave and throws it inside. An animal carcass falls at my feet. *Here, I got you some breakfast.*

The carcass is bigger than me, and my eyes widen in delight over the size of the hide. "Thank you, Elan. It's perfect in every way."

She gives me a strange look. *Okay. Whatever you say. It's just an animal. You need to share, though.*

I gaze back at the carcass and chuckle. "Do you expect me to be able to eat all of that?"

Her shoulders rise in what looks like a shrug. *You never know. You could work up a big appetite because of all the trouble you get into.*

I grab my sword and get to work skinning the carcass, making sure I don't nick the hide. Once I finish the lengthy ordeal, I throw it into the salty solution with the other one then wash the blood off my hands and arms. I cut off a hunk of meat and place it on a flat rock in front of Elan. "Can you please cook it for me?"

She gives me a strange look. *I don't know why you insist on burning it. Just eat it raw—it tastes better that way.*

"I prefer my meat dead and without blood, thank you."

Okay. Whatever you say. She breathes fire over the piece, filling the cave with the heat until the meat turns a nice dark brown. I wash my sword in the salty solution and cut the meat into bite-size pieces.

"You know, dragon-cooked meat is quite nice. It's surprising, really." I sit at the entrance of the cave, gazing out into the sunlight as I eat.

What else did you expect? Did you think it would taste like meat breath or something? Elan says sarcastically.

"Yeah. Meat breath means bad breath, so that would mean bad tasting meat."

Elan rolls her eyes, and I chuckle.

I spot her eyeing what remains of the carcass. "Help yourself to the rest."

Her eyes light up, and she wanders over and swallows it after a few chomps.

As we eat, I stare across the wilderness, observing Bifrost crossing the sky in a beautiful aurora of lights shining like rainbow beams from the sun. The colors break and gather then straighten again.

"There must be another reaping happening," I say, watching as it repeats this sequence. I'm tempted to jump on Elan's back and ask her to charge for Heimdall's Tower, but there is no point trying, especially right now. I would only be sent back to Asgard or imprisoned. Even so, I can't help wondering about Harut, the unusual angel of death I met briefly on Midgard, and whether he would be there, fighting the winged Valkyries for the souls of the dying warriors so he could take them to the underworld. Our brief encounter had been a strange one, and the angels of death should be my enemy. Instead, he had shown support for my cause because I was different from the other Valkyries he had met.

I push him from my mind and focus on life in front of me. "Is your mother back?" I ask, not seeing her among the siblings.

I haven't seen her. She must be checking everything out and discovering all the information she can.

A large cloud of worry crowds my mind. "You don't think she would have been caught, do you?"

Elan casts me a disbelieving look. *Um, seriously? Have you met my mother? Like she's going to let herself get caught. It's not like she's going to lie there and forget to make herself invisible and get caught, like someone else I know.* She rolls her eyes and shakes her head, and I know these gestures are aimed at herself. *Especially with the warning you've given her.*

"Well, you never know. Someone else was silly enough to do it." I lay a hand on her front leg, and she puffs out a stream of smoke. Her eyes dart my way, and I flinch from the sharpness. "You know I'm kidding, right? It wasn't your fault that you got kidnapped. Odin didn't give us any warning."

Yeah. I know. But it doesn't make it any less embarrassing. That's twice you've saved my life now.

"I'm sure you'd do the same for me." I say, shoving another lump of meat in my mouth. The Bifrost splits then straightens again, undoubtedly with another group of Valkyries taking off to Midgard.

I let out a deep sigh before swallowing the lump of meat. *How do I get myself out of this predicament?*

~~~~~

A FEW DAYS pass, and there is still no sign of Eingana. A deep churning knot worries my stomach. I hope she's okay. I know she's a big, bad dragon and all, but Odin is tricky.

To fill the time and occupy my mind, I set to work on the hides of the animals that Elan has been bringing me. At least twice a day, she supplies me with another animal—each one, I skin then soak their hides in the salty solution. If I stay out here any longer, I will have enough hides to make the things I need. I finish the tanning process, following the steps I learned at the Valkyrie academy.

We are responsible for making and fixing our own leather uniforms and other protection for our skin. Alongside this, we learned how to make more quivers for when others become worn out. I found that kind of work relaxing, a welcome break from all the bickering with the winged Valkyries and menial tasks set for the wingless Valkyries. I lack the tools that were available to us at the academy, but I will improvise. My sword proves useful for cutting the material, and I source a sharp, pointed rock to jab holes into the leather so I can thread the pieces together. Thankfully, Elan hasn't been tearing the hide too much with her teeth. They would be ruined if she had been biting them across the middle.

First, I cut the leather into long, thin pieces and plait them to make them stronger and thicker. The first thing I need to make is a bridle. Each time Elan enters the cave, I measure and fashion the ties around her head, shoulders, and waist. When complete, I set to work on the medium pieces of leather, fashioning a saddle.

Each day Elan brings me more hides, I am thankful. It will take a lot to fashion a sturdy saddle and enough straps to reach around her large waist.

When I'm satisfied with my progress on the saddle, I set to work making myself a leather cape. I cut and measure the sleeve to reach to my wrists and fall slightly over my hands. I make sure the leather of the cloak falls to my ankles, and I fashion a hood to pull over my head. I am determined to keep out the cold from the altitudes. Then I sew the golden scales from the hem of the cloak to the edge of the hood and sleeves. There is a large collection of scales available circling the emperor dragons' precipice—I have plenty. As I sew, I smile to myself. In this cloak, I will blend in with Elan when I am riding on her back. Once finished, I try it on and stroll in front of Elan.

Well, look at you. You almost look like a miniature dragon but without the nasty teeth and fire.

Pride fills my chest, and I can't help but parade in front of her a few more times.

I don't know if she picks up on my pride or if she means it: *What you've made is completely awesome.*

"Do you think that it will hold against a sword?" I spread it out wide, looking it over as I pose in front of Elan.

I don't know. Let's see.

I take the jacket off and hang it over a rock, spreading it out with the scales facing out. Pulling my sword from its sheath, I swing it directly at the scaled area. A loud clatter sounds, and the sword bounces away, letting the full force hit my sword. I drop the sword when the vibrations rattle up my arm. I dash to the cloak and have a look at the scales that I hit. Not one of them is dented.

"Look at that, Elan!" I can't contain my excitement. "This may even be stronger than a shield. What's even better, it protects more of my body."

And that is worth its gold! It even looks like me.

I weave my arm back through the sleeves of the cloak right as a heavy thump sounds outside.

I glance out into the sunlight and see a brilliant-red dragon standing not far from the entrance of the cave.

I still smell Valkyrie blood. This cannot be from Elan several days ago. Ness lifts her nose to the air and breathes in deeply. *In fact, the Valkyrie blood reeks stronger than before. Where is she?*

- CHAPTER SEVEN -

The red eyes scan the area and stare straight into the cave. *I can smell her. Let her out! Let me get to her! I'll rip off her limbs one at a time.*

Sobek moves discreetly into the space between Ness and the cave. *Isn't that a bit drastic?*

After what they've done to our younglings, that's what they deserve. They have enslaved my youngling for over a year, and she is treated terribly.

I'm sorry to hear that. Despite the threat, Sobek sounds sympathetic. Still, he does not move from standing between us.

I tuck myself behind a rock and pull my scale cloak over me. A crack between two rocks leaves just enough space to peer through and see what is going on.

The red dragon prances in front of the cave, her long red tail whipping behind her. *Where is she?*

Her footsteps become more impatient, and she stomps back and forth in front of the entrance, her nose twitching as she sniffs the air. *The Valkyrie reek is strong. Let her out. I need to get my claws on her.*

Elan casts me a glance, noticing that I'm squatting under cover of the scales and rocks. She strolls out of the cave and chuckles. *Oh, Ness. I don't know what you're talking about. It's just me.* She pauses at the entrance, blocking it from the red dragon with Sobek. *I know I've been hanging around the Valkyries way too much. Here, I can prove it.* She moves closer and tilts her wing, shoving the spot where she had been cradling me earlier in Ness's face.

The red dragon gives her a strange look.

Here, smell this. It reeks, doesn't it?

Ness screws up her nose.

See? It's just me. I've been spending way too much time in the Valkyrie area, trying to sort out this alliance and stop what is happening to the younglings. I'm so sorry to hear about your daughter. She shoves her wing in the red dragon's face some more. *But this smell is just me. It happens every time I go. I've just come back again, and I been sitting inside that cave, which makes it impossible for the fresh air to push away the smell of the Valkyries.*

The red dragon's nose screws up tighter. She pulls her snout away from Elan's underwing and snorts a puff of smoke followed by a blast of fire as she sneezes. *That's an awful stench. Have a bath, for dragon breath's sake! Or do you love the smell of Valkyries so much that you can't stand to wash it off?* She exposes her teeth in a sneer.

What? Do you think I bathe myself in Valkyrie smell? I'd rather roll in dragon manure—and I have tried to wash it off. It doesn't go away. The oils from their skin stick to me.

Even though Elan sounds convincing, Ness's suspicions don't leave her face. *You're just a Valkyrie lover. You and your family worship the ground they stand on.*

Elan sits upright, looking put out. *I beg your pardon? I'm not a Valkyrie lover. Even so, certain Valkyries aren't as bad. I've met a few. They are the ones without the wings. They don't fight against us to hurt our dragons.*

Liar! Ness sneers. *You're just a liar. You have been smooching up to these Valkyries and looking after your own family. You don't have to hand over any of your younglings. That's not fair!*

Elan puffs up her chest and pulls her shoulders back. *Do you realize who you're talking to? You should be showing me respect. I am second in charge of all these dragons, and you should be bowing down to me and doing as I say.*

Ness sneers, and she prances in front of Elan and Sobek. *Right! That's not going to happen. Just because you are born with golden blood does not make you a leader. You have to earn your right by fighting for it.* She spins on a heel, her eyes challenging. *If you think you're so high and mighty, then fight me to prove it.*

Sobek stands tall, his massive frame towering over both the female dragons. *Hang on. Those aren't the rules. Elan is second in charge and the one to be obeyed when Mother is away. You can't fight her. You have to do as you're told.*

Make me! Ness pulls back her top lip, revealing her pointy teeth.

Sobek moves toward her, and she lashes out, striking him across the face with her claws. Crimson blood runs from his face and tarnishes his golden scales. She had run her talons through the underside of his scales. *There. That proves it. You bleed just like the rest of us. There is nothing special about you or your blood.*

Elan rises from her haunches and stands defiantly. *You will not treat my family this way.* Anger radiates from her every scale, showing off her impersonation of her mother, which I have witnessed a few times now. Each time is just as intimidating as the last. During moments like these, I can see why Elan is the next in line to rule the dragons. She may be born of the blood, but she has every bit a leader lying deep within her despite her talkative and friendly nature.

I don't want her to fight. I don't want her to get hurt. I don't want any of them to get hurt, but there is nothing that I can do right now to stop the inevitable. I feel like a coward hunkered down behind boulders, peering out between the cracks and remaining cloaked inside my scaled gown. *Please don't let this happen*, I say to myself over and over, wishing it to go away. But as I do, Elan lashes forward and scratches Ness the same way that the red dragon had scratched Sobek.

Ness throws her head forward, letting out a deep growl accompanied by a large plume of fire aiming straight for Elan. Elan turns and shelters herself with her scales while spreading her wings high, spinning around until she hooks Ness, slashing her face with the claws on the edge of her wings.

Ness pulls her head back, and Elan takes the opportunity, tilting her head down and charging at the red dragon with her horns pointing forward. Ness darts to the side and lashes out with her claws as Elan runs past. The talons fail to dig past the scales, leaving Elan unscathed.

Elan spins around with bared teeth and charges for Ness's wing. The red dragon darts to the side, using her wings as leverage, and Elan's teeth connect near her shoulder.

Elan bites down, clasping and piercing the membrane of the wing. She shakes her head and rips holes into the upper wing as well as gashes in the shoulder of the other dragon.

Ness bellows, and it echoes down the valley and across the wastelands. I can't see the dragons down there, but I can imagine every head turning toward the cliff face. It's not the kind of attention I want up here.

Ness's teeth remain exposed, and she lashes her head around and sinks them into the side of Elan's neck. The sharp, pointy tips of Elan's scales shoot into Ness's mouth and pierce the inside of her mouth. It doesn't stop her from clamping her teeth down deeper into Elan's side.

The combined blood of two dragons pours down and splashes onto the ground, leaving crimson puddles. I want to call out and tell them to stop, but that would just put Elan in more danger because it would prove her a liar and show that she is sheltering a Valkyrie. I don't want any more harm to come to any dragons. I want peace in the land, not a dragon fight.

Elan twists her body and scratches her claws into Ness's underbelly. At the same time, she swings her tail around and hits the red dragon on the head, knocking it enough to make her let go. Ness bellows in agony, unclamping her jaws at the same time, setting Elan's neck free.

Oh, Vanir! I am so worried. What happens if Elan loses? My mind ticks over all the possibilities.

Sobek moves to step in, and Elan screams, *Don't you dare! This is my fight!* The brother halts and watches, his face contorted with anguish that deepens as Ness pounces and digs her teeth deep into Elan's neck.

- CHAPTER EIGHT -

The ground rumbles, and a menacing roar thunders through the cave and down the valley, more profound than either dragon has managed to expel thus far.

I cringe, hoping it's not a dragon from the valley, an older dragon who knows how to fight better than the dragons in front of me. The urge is strong to dart around and see who it is, but I can't afford to expose myself. These dragons scare me at the best of times, and the last thing I need is to be a small meat sandwich between ten or more dragons several sizes bigger than me.

The two fighting dragons halt then stagger to stand straight. They pull their eyes from each other as they search for the invading dragon.

The ground bumps and rattles as a big dragon stomps its way toward the two fighters. *What is the meaning of this?*

I breathe a sigh of relief. It's Eingana, the leader of the dragons—she has finally returned. A sense of safety fills me as she stomps toward the two dragons, her teeth showing in a full nasty growl.

Sobek approaches her. *Ness flew down and demanded to know where the Valkyrie smell was coming from.* His voice is humble and hesitant, and his eyes flick toward the cave. *Elan proved that the scent is from her because the stench has clung to her scales from spending so much time with the Valkyries.*

He glances at the dragons one by one, finishing with Ness, then he continues. *Ness did not believe her, despite the awful stench clinging to Elan's body. Elan even shoved her underwing in Ness's face.*

His mouth tilts up slightly into a quirky smile for a moment, but it quickly disappears. Eingana watches him intently, and I am sure that she noticed.

Sobek continues, *Ness did not believe Elan and challenged her position as second in charge of the dragons in the area. Elan did not strike first, Ness did.* He indicates the gash on the side of his face. *This is proof.* He raises his chin high. *It is after this that Elan jumped in to prove her honor, as you were absent, Mother.*

Eingana stares at the red dragon, back to Elan, then back to the challenger. *Ness, is this true?*

Ness stares at the ground and doesn't answer.

I take this as a yes. I hear that you have a substantial nest. You have five eggs about to be hatched.

A look of dread crosses Ness's face, and her eyes flick up to Eingana, the redness in them spreading to her whites. It is like the spread of a contagious disease taking over her.

Because of your actions, you will be handing over your firstborn from the hatch. You will have to give from your babies to take another red dragon's place this year.

She appears to be in shock. *No. Please, no. I sacrificed one of my babies only last year. They have been mistreating my baby. There must be another dragon ready to give away one of their babies.*

You have no one but yourself to blame for this. Eingana pulls her shoulders back, and her voice remains strong. *You have not obeyed our rules, and this is your punishment. I have the final decision over any of the other tribes if a particular dragon disobeys my ruling, and this you have done. The decision is final.*

No. Please, no! Ness falls to her knees and begs.

Let this be your lesson. Eingana turns her back to the red dragon. *Now leave.*

The terrified look does not leave Ness's face even as she bends her knees and pushes off into the sky. Her flight is lopsided from the injury caused to her wing. The damage was not so significant that she can't fly, but it stops the wing catching the air completely. Although it will heal in time, she will never be a fully functioning dragon again. Ness has learned the hard way. Even though it is my blood she was after, I still feel pity for her because I understand her plight.

Sobek runs up to Elan. *Are you all right?*

Eingana stomps up, observing Elan's injuries. *She shall live. She'll be sore for a bit, but she will heal. It is part of being the leader of the dragons.*

I don't hear much sympathy in her voice, but I guess that is what she has become, a tough leader in any circumstance, cutting away the emotion of what happens to make level decisions. *Is the Valkyrie okay?*

Elan and Sobek both nod. *Yes*, Elan says. *She hides in the cave.* She tilts her head toward the cave, and Eingana turns around to look inside.

I don't see her.

She is hiding, and she's hiding in an extraordinary way. A quirky pride fills Elan's voice. *You can come out now, Kara. Show Mother what you've made.*

Leaving my hood over my head, I emerge in my scale cape. Eingana tilts her head to the side as she watches me step out into the sun. The golden scales on my cape glitter in the sunlight.

Interesting. What is it? she asks.

"It's a cape. It has a leather lining that will protect me from the cold when I'm on Elan's back and when she takes me into the clouds. That altitude makes it chilly for me." I open the cape to show off the inner leather lining then close it to show off the neatly attached scales. "It is also a shield. I won't have to carry that big bulky thing I used back at the academy when I need protection in a fight or if they ever let me help protect them during the reaping. I can just keep this with me. As you know, your scales are tough, and it is hard for anything to penetrate their protection."

Ingenious. Eingana nods in approval.

Silence hangs in the air, and I wait for her to say something, but she doesn't. My impatience grows. "Is there any news? Has anything changed at the academy? Are my friends okay? We were so worried about you. You took so long that we had thought you had been captured or something."

She snorts out some smoke. *That's not going to happen!*

"You know Odin can be quite persuasive and aggressive."

He will achieve nothing if he tries to harm me. He may be a god, but that doesn't stop me making him my lunch. Eingana lifts her chin.

So what happened, Mother? Elan's brow creases. *Did you manage to fix anything?*

A look of pride passes across her face, and she nods. *As a matter of fact, I did.* The mother glances at me. *Kara's friends were impounded under Odin's Palace. He did not forgive them despite their innocence and the fact that they were only taking the dragon for a quick ride before bringing him back. It took me several days, but I managed to track down Loki and demand an audience with Odin.* She frowns. *I wouldn't be surprised if Loki has been up to mischief. Over the last few years, he has been using his shapeshifting forms too many times. But for once, I demanded he use it for good and change into a dragon to help communicate with Odin. It was a meeting that Odin couldn't understand.*

Her mouth works up at the sides. *Loki has some interesting facts and theories. He has an amazing mind with what he thinks about and plans. He is a schemer, that's for sure. We will have to watch him.* She paces in front of me. *After a long talk with Loki, he transformed into god form to talk to Odin then back into dragon form so Odin would think that Loki's dragon form was the only way he could understand us. Through this discussion, I managed to get Kara's friends released. It was part of the bargaining. I don't think they have been received back into the academy very well yet, but that will come with time. Your friends are tough, especially the redheaded one, Hildr.*

"Oh, yes. She is." I nod.

What about the dragon alliance, Mother? Elan asks. *Did you manage to sort Odin out and put him in his place over demanding one of ours?*

It took some threatening, but yes, I did manage to get this sorted. He cannot have one of ours. We are still low in numbers. He is not happy about it, and I do not trust him, but he has no right to an emperor dragon. Unfortunately, the alliance remains the same. We must still give up one dragon of each breed every year.

What about Kara? Sobek asks. He had been standing so still that I had almost forgotten he was with us. *Can she go back yet? She won't be safe here. It's too hard to protect her in this little area. The dragons are way too wild to accept her being here. Being a Valkyrie is an extra reason for them to eat her for lunch.*

Eingana stares at me for a long moment. Something is lingering in her eyes that I am unable to decipher. She looks at Sobek. *The discussion of Kara was brought up, yes. I have proven that she was only doing what was right by sticking to the alliance. I mentioned that Elan's capture by Odin would have made me angry, and Kara was releasing Elan so that my wrath would not be brought down on the Valkyries or Asgard. Odin knows he is in the wrong, but he doesn't want to accept that Kara was right. He has agreed to let Kara come back.* Her eyes drop to the ground, and she looks troubled.

What is it, Mother? Elan spreads her wing, touching her mother's back.

She releases an agitated sigh. *I cannot guarantee Kara's safety or that she won't feel Odin's wrath if she returns to the academy. I'm afraid, not only because she is wingless but also because she is allied with the dragons, that it will cause her much grief among the Valkyries of the academy.* She turns to look at me. *It is up to you, Kara, if you want to risk it.*

I glance at Elan, Eingana, and then back at Elan before gazing at Sobek. They have done much for me in the last few days. The blood pouring off of Elan's wings catches my attention. I meet Eingana's eyes. "Is there anything here to help Elan heal better? I can only imagine those dragon bites will become infected over time if not treated properly."

Eingana shakes her head. *We do not have healers. We have to let our bodies heal on their own. That is part of living in the wilderness.*

"Then the decision is made for me. I must take Elan back and take her to the healer to get some proper treatment."

But what about your safety, Kara? Elan's scales wrinkle between her horns. *I can't go into the academy and protect you.*

"I know. I'm willing to take that risk. I will have my weapons with me at all times, and I will hang out with my two friends. I know that they will look out for me too." I look up into her golden-brown eyes and see worry flooding through them. I stand in front of her and stroke her snout. "Don't worry, my friend. For you, it's worth it."

- CHAPTER NINE -

I dash into the cave and pull out the completed saddle. It took me hours to complete, but I had plenty of time while I was waiting in the dragon wastelands. I thread the leather around Elan's front legs, loop it around her torso, and pull it tight before adding the strap for around her neck.

I stop, though. "I think I will leave your neck free for the moment. It needs time to heal.

I don't want the straps digging into your injuries. The straps around your front legs and torso should hold the saddle steady enough for now."

Elan is a fantastic guinea pig. She stands still, letting me thread the straps around her body without showing any signs of a dragon's arrogance. It's hard to believe that she challenged another dragon not that long ago. The only telltale sign is her silence and lack of chattiness. She is more sedate while holding the responsibility for my safety within her talons. She watches me as I work, peering over her shoulder and wincing every time the lead squashes one of her wounds.

When I finish securing the saddle, I stand in front of her and hold her snout gently in my hands. Her eyes look tired, and her shoulders sag. "Are you going to have enough strength to fly back?"

She yawns, and her hot breath surrounds me. *I'll be fine. I've just lost a little bit of blood. But don't worry — dragons are tough. It's not that big of a flight anyway.*

I study her a bit more. "If you say so. But I want you to stop anytime you are struggling." I climb up to the saddle, hook my feet in the stirrups, then pull the reins tight. "Do you promise to do that? I don't want you passing out on me or anything. The last thing I need is to crash to the ground because my dragon has passed out."

Oh, thanks for your concern. It just reeks from your voice. She chuckles, glancing over her shoulder.

"You know I mean it." I give her a stern look.

She chuckles harder. *Ow! That hurts.* She stops chuckling. *Of course I know you mean it. I was just messing with you.*

Sobek shakes his head at her. *That's Elan — always joking around. You would never know that she is next in line to be in charge of the dragons.*

And a good leader she shall be after much education… if she keeps her mouth shut, Eingana says, and I almost think I see a glint of mischief in her eyes.

I tap Elan's back. "Did your mom just joke?"

Oh, under there somewhere, she has a sense of humor, Elan says lightheartedly. *Occasionally, it comes through.*

"Where is your sister?" I ask.

She has gone down to the dragons to make sure there are no more disruptions over what has happened here, Eingana says. *She must also train to become the leader in case something happens to Elan, for she is the next in line.* She raises her chin proudly, and her voice returns to the usual seriousness that I know.

"Say goodbye to her for me." I pull tightly on the reins and check the stability of the saddle.

Eingana nods once.

I wrap the cloak around me to maintain the perfect temperature under the scorching sun. It surprises me how it is blocking out the intense heat yet still traps the correct amount of warm air within. With my feet tucked securely in the footholds, I lightly click my feet against Elan's sides.

I do a last check on the reins again and move my backside around in the saddle. The molded leather is comfortable. "Right. I think we're good to go, Elan."

She jumps to her feet, and I hang on tight. The leather rubs against my hands, but it is nothing in comparison to the pointy ends of the scales that were my only security before.

Right, let's do it, Elan says, uncoiling her wings and pushing off into the sky, heading in the opposite direction of the valley filled with dragons. Her strokes are labored until we rise above the clouds.

The flight home isn't long, but it seems to drag. I don't know what I'm going to face when I get there. I don't know if they're going to send me to Odin to be imprisoned. The fact that Odin won't guarantee my safety proves that he will not help or stand up for me. But thinking it over, I know it's asking too much to expect a god to admit that he was wrong. It would be a massive blow to his pride if the god of wisdom were to be publicly proven incorrect. I have no sympathy for him.

Elan flies higher, and the icy winds push up against my face, numbing my skin, yet my arms and body are warm. Despite my worries, I am elated that the cloak is working against the icy chill.

Elan descends below the cloud cover, and her body disappears from underneath me, leaving me sitting in the air on a saddle, holding the reins as I float closer to the ground.

When I spot the academy in the distance, my stomach churns wildly inside of me. Physically, my ride home was easy, but emotionally, not so much.

Elan lands firmly, and she stomps forward a few steps before halting. I dip as I feel her front legs bend so she's lower to the ground, allowing me to slide off. I swing my feet over her neck and slide to the earth below.

"Can you turn visible for a moment? It will be easier to get the saddle off you without aggravating your wounds."

Her golden scales form in front of me as she turns visible, and I unhook the saddle and tuck it under my arm. I stroke her side. "Wait here. I'm going to find the healer to get you some ointment."

Elan nods then turns invisible before I run inside with my saddle. I dash to my room.

Hildr sits on her bed. Her face is pale and filled with uneasiness, and her hair is exceptionally spikey, as though she has been rubbing it enough that it stands completely on end. Eir sits not far from her. Her usually peaceful face is also worried. I remove my golden cloak and throw it on my bed with the saddle. I'm surprised they haven't seen me yet.

"Who died?"

Both of them spring up to look at me. Eir squeals with excitement, and Hildr embraces me into a rough hug, her sword hilt hitting me in the process. "You're whole," Hildr whispers in my ear.

I reach down and move her sword to the side then return the hug. "What's going on here? Have you gone soft on me all of a sudden?" I laugh and pull myself away.

Hildr's eyes look at me in disapproval. "When do I go soft? I can't help it if I get upset because you've disappeared. I thought you might have been eaten by a dragon, for goodness sake."

"Nearly. Elan did protect me. Which reminds me, I have to go and get some ointment off Anita." I turn to leave the room.

"We're coming, of course." Eir charges after me, followed by Hildr.

"I didn't expect anything else," I call back to them. "On the way there, you can tell me everything that has gone on since I've been gone."

"Oh." Eir sounds stressed. "Mistress Sigrun really has it in for you."

I roll my eyes and shake my head. "Oh, please. When doesn't she have it in for me?"

"She's pretty peeved," Hildr agrees.

"Like that's something new! I'll deal with her in a bit."

We reach the healer's room, and it takes no time for us to convince the academy's healer, Anita, to give us some ointment. As we leave, she calls, "Kara, be careful! Mistress Sigrun is pretty peeved off."

"Not you too," I say. "Don't worry. I'll deal with her soon."

We run out to Elan, and I smother her wounds in the salve then kiss her on the nose.

The moment I set foot inside the academy walls, I hear the screech of mistress's voice, "Valkyrie! My office, this instant!"

- CHAPTER TEN -

I stop and look at my friends. "I'll see you guys later, okay? Only I can deal with this one."

"Good luck," Hildr says.

I follow the stomping mistress down the corridors and into her office. Medals and trophies line every wall, accompanied by statues of winged Valkyries—it's almost like a shrine for them. Candles burn in little circles in front of the figurines. I roll my eyes and enter the room, closing the door behind me. "Yes, Mistress." I use the most bored voice I can muster.

Mistress Sigrun yanks her tan leather jacket closed over her white T-shirt then dusts off her medium-blue-leather pants. She is wearing the winged Valkyrie uniform, causing me to think that she must have just finished leading one of their training sessions. Her stunning pale face is set in a frown, as it so often is when she looks at the wingless Valkyries. She lifts her chin and shakes her head, tossing her perfect golden locks over her shoulder. Her majestic white wings pull in close to her body before she plunks her bottom down in the chair and glares at me from across her stone desktop. "You have caused too much mischief in the academy."

"That's what you keep telling me, Mistress." I study my fingernails, noticing the dirt underneath them.

"You have stolen something from under Odin's nose, and he is peeved." Her tone rises as she observes my actions.

I pick out some of the dirt and let it fall to the floor. "Actually Mistress, I didn't steal the dragon. Odin stole her, and I rescued her." I sit back in the chair and cross my legs. "And Odin knows this." I know I am being much more defiant than normal. I can't help it. It is hard to respect someone who rules with discrimination.

"Young Valkyrie, you will be respectful with me and when you are discussing a god. Your lack of respect for authority is appalling."

"No, Mistress. I don't lack respect for authority. I lack respect for stupidity." I know I've done it this time, but they have taken it too far.

"Is that right? You're calling Odin and me stupid?" She stares at me, waiting for an answer that doesn't come. "That's it. You're on cleaning duty."

"Oh, the change." I roll my eyes. "What is it this time? Dragon cell cleaning again?"

"No." She rises to her feet and stomps around the other side the table, towering aggressively over me. "It's worse. You're on toilet cleaning duty."

My shoulders sag. She's right—it is worse. I would much rather clean up after dragons than clean up after Valkyries. "Really, Mistress? Can't it be dragon stalls again?"

"You deserve the worst punishment." She shoves a key across the desktop then turns and dusts off a statue. "You will find the cleaning cupboard just down the hall. Go! You are to start now."

"But Mistress, I have only just come back from an extremely tiring ordeal. Can't it wait till tomorrow?"

"No. It can't. You have a lot of work to do to make up for your stupidity and defiance."

I exhale loudly, grab the key, and turn to leave. "Whatever!"

I trudge down the hallway and find the cupboard and all the bathroom cleaning equipment. I collect the cleaning items labeled "bathrooms" and close the door. Searing pain shoots through my shoulder, so strongly that I almost drop the equipment. I pull back my sleeve. The pain is in precisely the same spot as the scar that the creature gave me a couple of years ago. I haven't seen the creature in days. Surely, it can't be lurking around the academy—it wouldn't fit within its walls. I cover the scar and rub it through the material. I'll have to ask Anita if there is a cure. The old woman I ran into in the wilderness comes to mind. *What did she say about the scar again? It was really strange.* I frown when it doesn't come back to memory. With a shake of my head, I trudge down to the first bathroom I find.

Slowly, I push the door open and peer inside. It looks like it hasn't been cleaned for a while. The room stinks.

Cautiously, I enter, and the urge to tiptoe is strong. I push back the door of the first stall and screw up my nose. I can't believe that this is an all-girls academy—the stench is lethal. It's even worse than cleaning the dragon stalls. Something dark lies on the ground. I don't even want to know what that is. *This is disgusting!*

I block my nose and hold my breath. I don't want to smell this. After slipping on the rubber gloves, it takes a while to gather the courage to begin the cleaning process. I bend my knees, ready to stoop to pick up whatever it is when I hear something behind me. I straighten and exit the stall only to come to face-to-face with Rota, Prima, and Mist. *Great! My archnemesis and her buddies. They have hassled me since my first year.* I have not missed their faces while stuck in the dragon wilderness. I roll my eyes. "What do you guys want?"

"I heard you were coming back today," Prima says with a sneer. "So we made sure that this was a suitable job for you. We may have nominated you for this job to Mistress Sigrun then set to work making sure you had a little extra to clean up." She indicates the several suspect dark patches in the room. "I hope you like our decorating."

Studying the dark patches and taking in the stench, I am sure that it is not chocolate. My mouth straightens into a thin line as I look at Prima. "If that's yours, you can pick it up."

"Oh, wingless! That is not going to happen." Rota moves closer. "That's what you second-class Valkyries are for. In fact, you should be cleaning that with your face, not a rubber glove."

She approaches me, and my arms move up instinctively, ready to fight. She looks at them and sneers. "You forget who we are."

Mist moves forward, and I reach out and slap her with a gloved hand.

"Eww!" She groans. "That's disgusting!"

As Mist distracts me from the front, Prima scoots forward and grabs my arms from behind. "It's swirly time."

Mist's pretty face screws up in disgust. "Getting your head flushed is gross."

Rota grabs one side of me and helps Prima drag me to the toilet. I twist and lash out with my feet, kicking them in the thighs. They cringe yet somehow manage to secure their grasp.

Mist cheers them on, "Let's make her ugly black hair wet and sloppy." She giggles.

With bared teeth, I stretch my neck to try and bite Rota's shoulder. She notices what I am doing before I can make contact. I try to do the same to Prima until someone clears their throat. It sounds too old to be Mist. Rota glances behind us then stops. Confusion flickers over her face.

I twist around, still in their grasp, and my jaw drops with disbelief. The old woman from the wilderness stands at the entrance of the bathroom. "Young Valkyries! What do you think you are doing?"

Prima and Rota drop my arms at the same time, and I shake free.

When no one answers her, the old woman approaches us. "This is not the way to treat each other. I know this young Valkyrie. I have met her before, and I consider her a friend."

I should be grateful that she has stopped my archenemies from dunking my head, but I am too caught up in confusion. "What are you doing here?" My scar starts to ache again, and out of habit, I rub the spot.

The old woman raises an eyebrow. "Ah, it is giving you trouble again, I see. Here, let me have a look." Her old feet move surprisingly quickly across the floor, and she yanks my uniform down from my shoulder, revealing my scar. She runs her hand over it, and a strange tingling sensation runs the entire length of the scar and down my arm. My body convulses briefly.

"What did you do?" I ask.

"Time will tell." She smirks. Her faded eyes land on the three winged Valkyries, one at a time. "Now, Valkyries. I would be leaving Kara alone if I were you." Without waiting for a response, she spins on a heel and leaves.

My mouth drops open. *What just happened?*

"Crazy old bat!" Prima spits then grabs my arms again, assisted by Rota.

"She is one crazy old lady. I hope I'm never like that," Mist says with a tone that is so vague that it can't be taken seriously. She twirls a strand of her blond hair in her fingers while staring at the empty entrance.

My attention is yanked away as they start to drag me in the direction of the toilet. No matter what I do, I can't break free. After all, they're both warriors with much more training than what we have been given. Strange sensations stir in my scarred arm. It doesn't stop, and it feels different than it did when the creature was around. *What did the old lady do?*

Rota yanks my scarred arm forward, and the toilet bowl seems to leer up at me. Twisting my arm in a final attempt, I manage to grasp hold of her, with my hand bracing myself from being shoved farther. Something wells within the scar tissue then shoots down my arm, out my hand, and into Rota.

My eyes widen. *What was that?*

Rota squeals and drops to the ground.

Prima drops my other arm, and her wide eyes stare at the unconscious Rota. "What did you do?" Her voice is barely a whisper.

For a moment, my feet feel glued to the spot. I glance at Prima, then at Mist, then finally down at Rota's still form. My jaw drops, and I bolt out the door.

The End

ACKNOWLEDGMENTS

I am touched by the enormous amount of support I have received from my immediate family. My husband has been a helpful first reader and at times been a wonderful motivator, with hints of ideas to help me through the blanks. The support from my three sons has also been overwhelming. They have put up with my head being in the clouds, thinking about the next plot twist or story for several years. Along with many hours spent working on my books and keeping in touch with my readers.

A big thank you to my extended family who support me being a book enthusiast.

A huge thank you to my editor, Kate Birdsall, her editing and writing tips, and my Proofreader, Vanessa L, for picking up the things we missed.

Thank you to all of my readers who have loved my work, and continue to read my stories. I would love for you to share your thoughts in a review on one or all of the following:

Amazon.com
Goodreads
Barnes & Noble
You can follow Katrina Cope at:

https://www.facebook.com/Author.Katrina.Cope

https://twitter.com/Katrina_R_Cope

https://www.goodreads.com/author/show/7265107.Katrina_Cope

https://www.katrinacopebooks.com

http://http://www.amazon.com/Katrina-Cope/e/B00F00JF9M/

Book 4 of Valkyrie Academy Dragon Alliance Series 'Inflicted' released September 2019.

BOOKS BY KATRINA COPE

~~~~~

Pre-Teen Books

THE SANCTUM SERIES

JAYDEN'S CYBERMOUNTAIN

SCARLET'S ESCAPE

TAYLOR'S PLIGHT

ERIC & THE BLACK AXES

ADRIANNA'S SURGE

~~~~~

Young Adult Urban Fantasy

AFTERLIFE SERIES

FLEDGLING

THE TAKING

ANGELIC RETRIBUTION

DIVIDED PATHS

<u>Afterlife Novelette</u>

THE GATEKEEPER

~~~~~

Young Adult Urban Paranormal Fantasy

SUPERNATURAL EVOLVEMENT SERIES

(Associated with the Afterlife Series)

WITCH'S LEGACY (#0.5 Prequel)

AALIYAH

~~~~~

Young Adult Fantasy Nordic Myths

VALKYRIE ACADEMY DRAGON ALLIANCE

SERIES

MARKED (Prequel)

CHOSEN

VANISHED

SCORNED

INFLICTED

EMPOWERED

AMBUSHED

WARNED

ABDUCTED

BESIEGED

DECEIVED

GET UPDATES & NOTIFICATIONS OF GIVEAWAYS

Would you like a FREE copy of Marked?
Visit here:
https://www.katrinacopebooks.com/valkyrie-academy-dragon-alliance
Through this link you can sign up for my newsletter and receive a FREE copy of Marked plus updates about my fantasy books, sales and notification of giveaways.

DID YOU ENJOY THIS BOOK?
YOU CAN MAKE A BIG DIFFERENCE.

Honest reviews of my books help bring them to the attention of other readers.

If you've enjoyed this book, I'd be grateful if you could spend a few minutes leaving a review (it can be as short as you like).
The review can be left on Amazon and Goodreads.
Thank you very much.

ABOUT THE AUTHOR

Katrina is an author of several Young Adult and Preteen/Middle Grade novels. Each of her released books reaching the top 100 in certain categories on the Amazon's Best Sellers Rank – a few even as high as number one.

She resides in Queensland, Australia. Her three teenage boys and husband for over nineteen years treat her like a princess. Unfortunately though, this princess still has to do domestic chores.

From a very young age, she has been a very creative person and has spent many years travelling the world and observing many different personalities and cultures. Her favourite personalities have been the strange ones, yet the ones under the radar also hold a place in her heart.

During her last extensive travels, she spent 16 nights in a bomb shelter on a Kibbutz 8 kilometers off the Lebanese border. It was to avoid Katyusha bombs that the resident volunteers decided to name her after (she is still trying to work out why).

Katrina's online home is at
www.katrinacopebooks.com

You can connect with Katrina on:

Twitter https://twitter.com/Katrina_R_Cope

Facebook https://www.facebook.com/Author.Katrina.Cope

Instagram https://www.instagram.com/katrina_cope_author

Pinterest https://www.pinterest.com.au/katrinacope56

Email authorkatrinacope@gmail.com